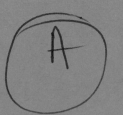
E
MOSER, Barry
The tinderbox

DATE DUE

322

once.
for each

book is
ayment of

KEEP YOUR CARD IN THIS POCKET

DEMCO

THE TINDERBOX

Hans Christian Andersen

THE TINDERBOX

Adapted, illustrated, and designed by

BARRY MOSER

Little, Brown and Company
Boston   Toronto   London

For Kay, with love and affection.

First edition

Library of Congress Cataloging-in-Publication Data

Moser, Barry.
 The tinderbox / Hans Christian Andersen ; adapted
and illustrated by Barry Moser. — 1st ed.
  p. cm.
 Summary: A retelling of Andersen's classic tale of a
brave soldier who finds love and fortune in a magic
tinderbox.
 ISBN 0-316-03938-1
 [1. Fairy tales.] I. Andersen, H. V. (Hans Christian),
1805–1875. Fyrtojet. II. Title.
PZ8.M8464Ti 1990
[E]—dc20   90-30279
                                                  CIP
                                                   AC

10 9 8 7 6 5 4 3 2

HR

Published simultaneously in Canada
by Little, Brown & Company (Canada) Limited
Printed in the United States of America

THE TINDERBOX

THE WAR was over. A young soldier was returning home when, high in the mountains, his path came to an end at a precipice. From here there was nothing more than a treacherous ledge of sandy rocks jutting out from the mountainside. So he stood, crestfallen, staring into the vast, misty space, afraid. He pushed on, though, until the ledge narrowed so much that he had to walk sideways. His pack and fiddle were heavy and cumbersome, so, reluctantly, he dropped them into the silent abyss. All he kept was his satchel containing a few meager rations, a pipe, and three copper coins.

When the ledge widened enough for him to walk normally, he saw the figure of an old man silhouetted in the thick, gray mist.

"Excuse me, sir, may I pass?" the soldier asked politely.

The old curmudgeon said nothing.

The soldier repeated his question, which was barely out of his mouth when the old man demanded, "Who are ya? Whaddya want? What're ya doin' on my mountain?"

The young soldier recoiled from the rasping voice and nearly fell over the edge.

"N-n-name," he stammered, "is Yoder Ott, sir."

Another long, silent pause.

"Yoder Ott?" the old man mumbled. "Well, Yoder Ott, if'n ya wanna go 'long this path, ya gotta do something for me first."

"Why should I...Why should I do anything for you, old man?" Yoder said, trying to regain some of his confidence.

" 'Cause it'll make ya as rich as Croesus, boy," the old man said in a matter-of-fact sort of way.

This interested Yoder very much, because not only was Yoder Ott a tired and tattered soldier, he was a poor one, too.

"See 'at stump up thar?" the old man asked, pointing upward with a wriggling finger, not taking his eyes off Yoder.

Yoder cranked his head back and looked up.

"Yes," he said.

"Uh-huh. Waal, just above 'at stump's a hole. Ya climb up thar with the end of this here rope. Put it around the pulley, then tie y'self to it. I'll lower ya to the bottom of the hole from down here."

"Then what?" asked Yoder, knowing there had to be more to getting rich than climbing rocks and going into caves.

"Git money," the old man answered simply, picking at the fingernails on his gnarled hand, not looking at Yoder.

"Oh?"

"It's easy, Ott," the old man said. "When ya git all the way to the bottom, ya gonna find three doors—now listen up good, boy—behin' each o' them doors ya gonna find a great big dawg what's got big eyes an' big teeth a'sittin' on top of a wood casket."

The old man paused in the middle of his instructions to untie his leather apron and slip it off over his head. He handed it to Yoder, and said, "Ya open 'at first door, honey boy, an' take this here apern an' put it on the floor. Then ya lift 'at dawg off'n the casket an' set 'im on it. Won't hurt ya none—not if ya do it jus' like I tell ya to.

"Now...when he's on the apern, ya open that'ere casket—'cause that's where the money is...copper money, boy—an' ya kin take all of it ya kin carry.

"Or," the old man said, twisting his whiskers with his fingers, one eye all squinted up, "ya kin go to t'other door, the one right near the first'un. Behin' it ya gonna fin' 'nother dawg, an' this'n's eyes're bigger'n the

9

first'un's. Do the same 'xact thing: lay the apern on the floor an' put the dawg on it. Casket he's a'sittin' on's full of *silver* coins.

"Or"—he paused a moment, working at his nails some more—"if silver ain't good enough fer ya…go to the door 'top them steps. In thar, ya gonna find 'nother casket with a dawg a'sittin' on it—an' he's got eyes bigger'n either one o' them first two. Put him off, too, just like 'em others…an' I tell ya this, boy, *his* casket's got GOLD in it—more'n ya kin carry.

"Now…," the old man continued, "when ya got all ya kin tote, gimme a holler, an' I'll pull ya up."

"And what do you get out of this, old man?" asked Yoder, knowing that no one ever gets something for nothing.

"All's I want," he replied pleasantly, admiring his newly cleaned fingernails, "is a tinderbox my ol' grandma left down thar a long time ago. It's kinda like one o' them fam'ly air-looms, ya know what I mean?"

"Yes. But is that all?"

"That's all, honey boy."

"Okay, then, I'll do it." With that said, Yoder grabbed the end of the old man's rope and began climbing up the mountainside with it. When he got to the stump, sure enough, there was an opening. Leaning out from the opening, he passed his end of the rope over the pulley wheel, and then tied it around his waist. He sucked in his courage, and hollered down that he was ready. The old man began lowering him into the dark dampness. Yoder was afraid. He could see nothing but pitch blackness. He could hear nothing, either—nothing, that is, but the thumping of his heart and the steady dripping of water. He tried to calm himself by imagining what he would buy if he were rich: a new fiddle, of course, and new clothes. New boots. Books. Some things for his folks—a new barn, maybe, a team of good mules. Some play pretties for his little sister, Serena.

The bottom came up suddenly—*thump*—and Yoder went sprawling on the wet floor. He could see light now—bright, amber light. There were ancient columns and statues supporting a low stone ceiling. He unhitched the rope, wondering what the columns were holding up…the

mountain? Then he saw the three doors—huge wooden doors with rows and rows of iron studs and long iron hinges. Two of the doors were on the floor and one was above the others with stairs leading up to it.

Yoder looked around apprehensively as he approached the first door. It had odd, curlicue letters painted above it and Yoder studied them for a long while before he made them out: O R V I S.

"Orvis?" Yoder whispered slowly, trying to pronounce each letter and wondering what the word might mean.

There was a key hanging beside the door. Yoder took it off its rusty iron hook and inserted it in the lock. Slowly the door groaned open.

Yoder fell back with a gasp at what he saw.

It was just as the old man had said it would be: a huge dog was sitting on top of a large wooden casket, panting and staring at the soldier fiercely with wild green eyes. Yoder had never seen a dog like him. He was the size of a small calf. His breath was hot and his eyes were huge, or seemed as if they were, anyway, certainly as large as…"as…as SAUCERS," Yoder stammered out loud, struggling for a description.

He remembered the letters above the door. Perhaps they spelled this creature's name, Yoder thought. He pronounced them again, this time stammering with fear: "O-O-Orvis?"

Immediately, the dog's tail thumped the chest and his eyes smiled. Then Yoder did as he had been instructed. He laid the old man's leather apron on the stone floor, took hold of Orvis, lifted him—stumbling backward with the huge dog's weight—and put him, feet down, on the apron. Orvis circled it once or twice, lay down, and went to sleep.

Yoder turned toward the casket. He lifted the lid and it yawned open. Inside, just as the old man had said there would be, were copper coins. More than he had ever seen. He stood before the treasure, wide-eyed with disbelief. Then he began to fill his pockets—quickly, as if he were pressed for time. He took off his boots and filled them, too. Then, when he had as much as he could carry, he closed the casket and hoisted Orvis back on top of it. He patted the great dog on the head, backed out of the room, and shut the door.

With his pockets and boots full of copper, Yoder tottered to the second door, which was just like the first one, with iron studs and hinges. It had letters written above it, too, and a key hanging beside it. These letters read Y O U L I E.

"You-LIE, YOU-lie," Yoder whispered, trying different pronunciations as he took the key from its hook and opened the door. It groaned like the first one did as Yoder pushed against it and went in. Sure enough, just as the old man had said there would be, there was a large wooden casket with a massive, saggy-faced dog sitting on top of it—the size of a pony. Her breath was hot and her eyes were fiercer and larger than Orvis's. They seemed as large as... "as...as...as wagon wheels!" Yoder exclaimed. He tried the name to see if it worked the way it had with old Orvis.

"YOU-lie?" he asked.

At the sound of her name, Youlie smiled and wagged her tail. Since this dog was so much larger than Orvis, Yoder knew that there was no way he could possibly lift her off the casket. So, after standing and scratching his chin for a while, trying to solve the problem, he asked Youlie— politely—if she would just hop down and sit on the old leather apron. Youlie tilted her head first to the right, then to the left, then obliged the young soldier by doing exactly as she was asked.

Yoder approached the casket and opened it.

To his amazement, it *was* full of silver—just as the old man had said it would be.

He quickly dumped all his copper onto the floor and started replacing it with silver, yelling, "I'm *rich!* I'm RICH! I'm RICH!" He threw silver coins into the air. Then, slapping his hand to his mouth as if he had discovered a secret, he whispered to himself, "I'd be richer still, if all this were *gold.*"

Excitedly, Yoder finished filling his pockets. "Who knows," he thought, "that old codger might by lying about there being gold." He closed the casket, and Youlie hopped back on top without even being asked. Yoder patted her on the head quickly and dashed heavily out of the chamber.

15

He made his way up the stairs to the third door, upon which the name ULYSS was lettered. He removed the key and unlocked the door. It swung open, and lo and behold! there on a casket sat a white dog bigger than either of the first two.

"My, my, Ulyss," Yoder said casually, listing into the room, "your eyes seem as big as . . . as windmills."

No sooner had he put the leather apron on the floor than the powerful dog jumped down and sat on it.

Yoder opened the casket with dispatch, and, to his wonder and joy, it *was* full of gold. Frantically, he dug into his pockets and flung his silver in the air, raining it down on everything, including Ulyss. When he had rid himself of silver, he stuffed everything he could with gold.

Then, as he was about to leave the chamber, he remembered his errand — to find the old curmudgeon's heirloom tinderbox.

"Now where do you think I'm supposed to find *that* thing?" Yoder asked himself, gold coins clinking out of his pockets. No sooner had he asked the question than he saw the small box beneath one of the ancient columns. "Was that there when I came in?" he wondered.

He waddled over to it, picked it up, and stuffed it into his tunic, which was already full and sagging with the weight of the gold. He made his way back to the bottom of the hole and hitched himself to the rope again. More coins spilled onto the floor. He hollered to the old man, "Pull me up!" and a moment later he began to ascend — slowly. On the way up he thought more about how to spend his gold, but he also wondered about the ancient columns, the three giant dogs, and how in the world the old man could have possibly heard him when he hollered for him.

When he was back on the treacherous ledge, Yoder asked the old codger, "What's so special about this tinderbox, old man? What're you going to do with it?"

"Gimme it!" the old man shouted hoarsely. "Ain't none of yer bidness."

"If you don't tell me, I'm going to keep it."

"Oh, no, ya ain't, ya little whippersnapper," the old man snarled as he lunged for the box.

Yoder stepped back, out of his way. The old man lost his footing, and fell...without a sound...into the cold, colorless abyss.

Yoder was rich now, and he owned a tinderbox that he was sure the old man had wanted for something other than lighting fires, though he was not at all certain what that might have been.

"Oh, well...it's mine now," he mused as he put the gold from his boots into the old man's leather apron. He was jubilant as he prepared once again to make his way home.

Night was falling just as Yoder crossed a notch in the mountain and found himself at the edge of a forest. He lay down, too tired even to eat, and fell sound asleep. He slept poorly, dreaming of his family and of home.

The next day Yoder pressed on through the forest and soon came upon an unfamiliar village nestled in the mountains. At first, he was angry and disappointed because now he knew that he was truly lost. But, he reasoned, since he was rich, he could afford anything a mountain hamlet would have to offer. So he decided that he would just settle in and then try to figure out how to get home.

He made his way down a dusty road to an inn; the Boarshead Inn, it was called. There, he rented the best rooms they had, ones with fine furnishings, with a bathtub in a room all to itself, and with a splendid view of the mountains. He had a bath, a good supper, and went to bed. This night he slept soundly.

Next morning, he deposited his gold in the bank and had the local haberdasher fit him out in fine clothes. He had the cobbler turn out a handsome pair of boots for him, and hired a bootblack to tend them. He bought books, and he bought a new fiddle.

Evenings, after a rich dinner, he repaired to his rooms and read his books and played music. He was very content.

Since Yoder was a rich man, the townsfolk paid attention to him and curried his favor. The merchants and vendors shared all the local gossip with him, and treated him as if he were a venerable member of their community. They told him about old Missus Priddy and about the Rever-

19

end Mr. Turnipseed. They told him about the town's mayor, the Honorable Odius Leon Abernathy, his wife, Ernestine Grace Abernathy, and their beautiful daughter, Elvira Abernathy.

"Oh, *really*? I'd like to meet her," Yoder said, confidently.

"That's impossible," the butcher told him, "because she hasn't been out of the mayoral mansion in five years."

"Only His Honor and his missus come and go from the mansion," the baker told him.

"Anyway, don't flatter yourself, young man," the banker told him, risking honesty, because he too had money.

"She *is* very lovely," the barkeep told him.

"She is *very* lonely," the bootblack told him.

Days passed. Weeks. Yoder put off trying to get home. After all, no one was expecting him. So he spent all his time reading, playing music, daydreaming about Elvira Abernathy, and spending his gold.

Of course, it wasn't long before his gold was all gone. He let his servants go and gave up his rooms at the Boarshead Inn. He moved into a cold garret above Sodergren's, the hog butchers, and paid his rent by scalding the butchered hogs and shaving off their stiff bristles. He played his fiddle at a local tavern, but people no longer respected him—he was as poor as they were, and he smelled of scalded pigs. Very few copper coins were pitched into his cap, barely enough to buy food. Eventually, he sold or traded everything he owned just to buy bread—everything, that is, but two books, and the meager things he had arrived with.

One evening, Yoder was reading. When there was no longer enough light to read by, he laid his book across his chest and stared at the ceiling. Then he remembered seeing a bit of candle in the old codger's tinderbox, and that, he reasoned, would give him enough light to read by for a little while longer. So he rummaged around and found the old metal box. He opened it and took out the candle end. Then he laid out a bit of tinder, and struck the flint across the box....

21

Bright sparks flew into the cold twilight air.

The door flew open, and there, in the hallway, stood Orvis. He lumbered into the room.

"What is it my master wants?" he asked in a voice that seemed to roll and grumble up from his belly.

Yoder was dumbfounded, and sat on his pallet mute with astonishment. "*Money,*" he thought.

"Mon—." He cleared his throat. Tried again.

"Money!"

Zzzip. Orvis disappeared.

Then:

Zzzip. Orvis reappeared with a large satchel full of money.

"Boy, what a great prize *this* thing is!" Yoder exclaimed, hugging the tinderbox to his chest.

It didn't take long for Yoder to find out that if he struck the tinderbox once, Orvis appeared, ready to grant whatever Yoder wished. If he struck it twice, Youlie would appear and likewise grant Yoder's slightest wish. If he struck it three times, Ulyss came to do his bidding.

Yoder asked for money over and over, became rich once again, and knew that he would never again be poor.

He rented back his fine rooms at the Boarshead Inn. He bought new finery for himself, some new books, a new bow for his fiddle—one made of gold and ivory. Once again his favor was curried, as that of someone special, by the bakers and bankers and butchers and booksellers.

Then, late one night, as he played his fiddle quietly, he wondered—as he often did—what Elvira Abernathy might be like. He imagined meeting her.

"Aha!" he exclaimed, snapping his fingers. "Maybe I can meet her after all!"

He got out his tinderbox and struck it three times. He needed Ulyss to do the job he had in mind.

Zzzip. Ulyss appeared in his chambers. "Yes, Mr. Ott? What can I do for you tonight, sir?"

"Ulyss, I want to see Elvira Abernathy."

No more was the *a* of "Elvira" out of his mouth than big Ulyss was gone—*zzzip*. And no sooner was he gone than he was back again, bearing Elvira on his back, sound asleep.

Yoder moved close and looked at Elvira. Indeed, he had never seen such beauty. Impetuously, he bent down and kissed her on the cheek, gently. Then, suddenly, his lips still puckered, *zzzip*...Ulyss and Elvira were gone.

The next morning as the mayor, His Honor Odius Leon Abernathy, his missus, Ernestine Grace, and Elvira were having their breakfast, Elvira told her parents about a strange dream she had had the night before: "I dreamed that I was carried away from the mansion on the back of a huge dog into the night sky, and to the quarters of a fine young man. He looked at me tenderly...and then...he...he kissed me, here, on my cheek." She blushed as she touched her cheek with her fingertips.

Her mother frowned knowingly at the mayor.

Later in the day, Ernestine Grace called upon Ruthenia Lowhorn, her sister-in-law, a woman knowledgeable in the ways of mountain magic. She asked Ruthenia to watch Elvira's chambers at night, and to report anything out of the ordinary. So it was; no one argued with Ernestine Grace.

Two days passed with Yoder lost in constant thought of Elvira. So, able to stand it no longer, he fetched his tinderbox and struck it again—two times—and summoned Youlie.

Zzzip. The huge dog appeared.

"Youlie," Yoder said, "I want to see Elvira again. Tonight."

No sooner had he said "Tonight" than it was done. Except that this time Elvira's midnight journey was observed from not far behind by the unseen Ruthenia Lowhorn, who saw Youlie deliver Elvira into the inn. She took a piece of chalk from her purse and drew a large cross on the front door.

"Now *anybody* will be able to find this place in the daylight," she said as she clapped her hands, dusting off the chalk.

The next morning, all was a-tither to see His Honor Odius Leon and his missus, Ernestine Grace, come to town. Their visits were rare in those days; usually they came to town only around election time. Of course, they came expecting to find the young soldier behind the door marked with the cross. But, unknown to Ruthenia Lowhorn, Youlie had observed the cross on her master's door and had marked every door in town with similar crosses.

The mayor, with his wife, his sister, and their entourage of selectmen and selectwomen, went back to the mayoral mansion. Ernestine Grace was greatly disappointed in Ruthenia Lowhorn and had her promptly put out of the mansion.

Now, Ernestine Grace was not a woman to give up easily. She made a small bag out of sackcloth, filled it with pumpkin seeds, and sewed it to Elvira's dressing gown. Then she cut a hole in the bottom of it, and went back to bed.

Later in the night Orvis came and fetched Elvira away, and took her back to Yoder's quarters. But poor Orvis, who was not as bright as Youlie, failed to notice the trail of seeds they were leaving behind. So, early the next morning, Ernestine Grace followed their path with ease.

Upon her orders, Yoder was yanked from his bed by the sheriff's men, arrested, and taken to the town jail. There was no indictment, no trial. Ernestine Grace simply told the mayor, her husband, to hang Yoder. "Hang him today," she demanded. And the mayor, henpecked as he was, resigned himself to comply.

So Yoder was thrown in jail—and once again had nothing—only his nightshirt and nightcap. His fine clothes and boots were gone, his books, his fiddle with its new bow, and his tinderbox....

"My tinderbox!" Yoder exclaimed, muffling half the sound with his hand over his mouth.

He pushed a stool over to the barred window of the cell and looked out at the street. Nearby, workers were building a gallows. The town was festive in anticipation of the hanging: banners and flags waved and danced in the clear noonday air. Yoder pulled himself closer to the bars and

watched the street for someone he knew, someone he could trust. Soon, Coy Lee, the young son of his bootblack, came running down the street.

"Coy Lee...up here," Yoder whispered loudly.

Coy Lee looked up and saw Yoder.

"How would you like to make some money, Coy Lee? Say, three pieces of silver?"

"Shore," came the reply. "Whadda I have to do fer it?"

"Go back to the inn and fetch me my tinderbox, my pipe, and my leather satchel."

"That all?" Coy Lee asked.

"That's all. But do it in a hurry, and don't let anybody see you."

The boy scurried away, darting in and out of the gathering crowd.

Before long he returned with the tinderbox, the pipe, the satchel, and threw them up to Yoder. Yoder caught them and promptly took three pieces of silver from the satchel. He tossed them down to Coy Lee, who disappeared before his voice faded, saying, "Oh, *boy!*"

At precisely that moment, the jailer, an old giant of a man, unlocked the door to Yoder's cell and ducked in. He had come to take the unfortunate soldier to the gallows, and had brought suitable clothing for him to be hanged in—trousers, a belt, a white shirt, stockings, and some uncomfortable boots.

The old jailer propped himself against the door and nodded off to sleep while Yoder dressed. He, of course, did not notice that Yoder put the tinderbox into the pocket of his trousers. When Yoder was fully dressed, he woke the old man up, and the two of them made their way to the gallows.

It seemed to Yoder as if the whole town had gathered. Vendors sold peanuts and marzipan, cotton candy and fried hog rinds. Children played hopscotch and jumprope, tag and pirates among the skirts and coattails of the men and women in the crowd. The mayor and his missus sat in the v. i. p. box talking with the selectmen and selectwomen.

The crowd was laughing and cheering as Yoder was led up the steps to the gallows. The hooded hangman placed the noose over his head.

"Don't I get a last request?" Yoder asked loudly, certain that the mayor would allow it. "Surely since His Honor did not allow me a trial, he will not let me be hanged without granting me one last wish."

"No!" said Ernestine Grace, bouncing in her chair.

"Hush!" said the mayor to his wife, surprising himself with his boldness. Ernestine Grace stopped bouncing. Then to Yoder he said, "Certainly you may, depending, of course, on what it is you wish."

"All I ask, Your Honor, is that I have one last smoke of my pipe."

"That all?" asked the mayor.

"That's all, sir."

The mayor folded his arms across his chest and granted the wish.

Yoder put the pipe in his mouth, took the tinderbox from the pocket of his trousers, and struck it—one…one-two…one-two-three. And in a *zzzip* of a flash, all three dogs materialized in front of the astonished crowd.

Yoder yelled out to the dogs, "Youlie, boys, don't let them hang me!"

Faster than anyone could see or imagine, the three dogs leapt upon His Honor and his missus. Then they turned on the selectmen and selectwomen, and then on the sheriff's men. (The old jailer was safely asleep under the gallows.) When the dust settled, the three dogs were standing by Yoder's side, and the people, ashamed that they had been about to stand by and watch an innocent and kind man be hanged, said with one voice, "Yoder, Yoder, you can be our mayor now…the mayoral mansion can be your home and you can marry Miss Elvira, too, if she'll have you."

And with that, the crowd carried Yoder on their shoulders to the mayor's wagon, whereupon he drove off down the road for the mayoral mansion.

Night was falling.

The three great dogs jogged ahead.